For Katherine

BEACH LANE BOOKS • An imprint of Simon & Schuster Children's Publishing Division • 1230 Avenue of the Americas, New York, New York 10020 • Copyright © 2010 by Alison Lester • Originally published in Australia in 2010 by Allen & Unwin • First U.S. edition, 2012 • All rights reserved, including the right of reproduction in whole or in part in any form. • BEACH LANE BOOKS is a trademark of Simon & Schuster, Inc. • For information about special discounts for bulk purchases, please contact Simon & Schuster Special Sales at 1-866-506-1949 or business@simonandschuster.com. • The Simon & Schuster Speakers Bureau can bring authors to your live event. For more information or to book an event, contact the Simon & Schuster Speakers Bureau at 1-866-248-3049 or visit our website at www.simonspeakers.com. • Book design by Lauren Rille • The text for this book is set in Plumbsky. • Manufactured in China • 0812 SCP • 10 9 8 7 6 5 4 3 2 1 • Library of Congress Cataloging-in-Publication Data • Lester, Alison. • Noni the pony / Alison Lester.—1st U.S. ed. • p. cm. • Summary: Introduces Noni the pony, who is friendly and funny and lives at Waratah Bay, where her best friends are Dave Dog and Coco the Cat. • ISBN 978-1-4424-5959-5 (hardcover) • ISBN 978-1-4424-5960-1 (eBook) • [1. Stories in rhyme. 2. Ponies—Fiction.] I. Title. • PZ8.3.L54935Non 2013 • [E]—dc23 • 2012004907

noni the pony

Alison Lester

BEACH LANE BOOKS • New York London Toronto Sydney New Delhi

Noni the pony is friendly and funny.
Her shimmering tail is the color of honey.

She lives on a farm at Waratah Bay,
and likes eating apples and carrots and hay.

Noni the Pony likes trotting and prancing,
and the ladies next door always moo while she's dancing.

She gallops and spins and canters and bucks,
then kicks up her heels with the hens and the ducks.

Noni the Pony is shiny and fat.
Her best friends are Dave Dog and Coco the Cat.

They ambush each other and play hide-and-seek,
racing and chasing and jumping the creek.

Noni the Pony is gentle and kind,
and never lets anyone get left behind.

If Coco and Dave feel lonely or gray,
Noni tells stories to brighten their day.

It's hard to give Noni the Pony a fright,
but once in a while, she gets spooked in the night.

When the leaves rustle and sigh in the breeze,
Noni thinks monsters are shaking the trees.

So at bedtime her friends snuggle in for a song...

then Noni the Pony sleeps tight all night long.